most of

A NOVEL

By Bella De La Rocher

ABOUT BELLA DE LA ROCHER

(Written in third person but still written by me)

Bella De La Rocher is a writer whom has written or started 28 books, 75 short stories, and 266 poems. She also has 23 scripts which can only be described as "Netflix-ready"TM.

But Bella is mainly and mostly the creator of a heart-stopping literary crime thriller novel in progress, which is this book. The novel stars Chauncy Nathaniel Swanston, a man whom manages to be both fictional and factual at once.

How so? you enquire.

Well because although Chauncy is, on the one hand, "not real", he is also, at times, the most corporal it is possible for a man to be. But only to Bella. You must remember that. Even though, as you read about him, you will think you know him and can access him — I'm sorry — you just can't. You'd do well to show a bit of restraint, to be honest.

Bella is also a freelance leaflet writer for the renown Colour Therapist (in the Doncaster area) Clifford H Valentine for whom she has penned the following publications: *Dye or Die,*

3

Shades of Glory, Tint your way out of sadness and *Which hue for a new you?* [probably available via mail order, but only if you know Cliff, sorry but Bella is just not prepared to put you in touch with him.]

As well as being alphabetically-gifted, Bella is also a very talented visual artiste. One of the things she can do really well is see faces in potatoes and then take photos of them. This ability does not stop at whole potatoes: she has also documented faces in potato peelings as well as meat, eggs, breads and clouds. Bella remains unclear about whether or not these faces are evidence of ghostual hauntings or if they are her ancestors communicating things.

When she is not writing or thinking about writing or channeling Chauncy, Bella can be found in her annex (which is NOT attached to her parents' house) surrounded by lava lamps and fantastic ideas.

INTRODUCTION

[to this book]

Hello and allow me to welcome you to my book, written by me: the writer Bella De La Rocher.

What I am doing on these pages is sharing my writings with you.

This book is A NOVEL in progress about CHAUNCY, the fictional man whom regularly visits me in the annex in which I dwell. I will tell you more about him in a bit, but for now it is enough for you know that my dalliances with him are intense, philosophical, and rapturous.

Since I became writer ('a' missed out on purpose) I have written probably thousands (if not more) creative works, from poems to short stories, to scripts for the theatre and radio, to ten-part dramas for Netflix, to essays and articles, to leaflets, to small advertisements in the 'for sale' section of the local paper.

"WOW Bella, you're so unappreciated in your own time!" you enthuse.

And I could not agree more.

MORE ABOUT CHAUNCY

Chauncy, whoms full name is Chauncy Nathaniel Swanston, first appeared to me at approximately 3.50am one winter's night in my annex, which is actually more like a studio apartment if I'm honest, surrounded by an almost supernatural *but in no way imagined* glow. He stood at the foot of my bed while requesting my help, mostly via his devastated eyes, which are green and framed by thick black eyelashes.

The reason he appeared was because his parents had been murdered and he wanted to find out whom had done it to them. Though I did not see mineself as writer at this time, Chauncy clearly did, and I believe this is the first <u>and only</u> known case of a fictional character sourcing its own writer.

Please, if nothing else you must realise this: I had never met this man before. I had never considered myself as writer before. Can you can imagine the effect this experience had upon me? A fictional creation of my own making from my own subconscious in my own annex asking for my help???

Well I handled it very well, thank you.

Basically Chauncy begged me to find out what happened to his murdered parents whom had been murdered a year ago to the very day. "Write my story, Bella, please!" he demanded kindly, urgently, vibratingly. "There is no time to lose! Let my story pour from me and then into you like honey, and then will you please pour THAT onto the page! But in word-form. Thanks. PS I don't want a girlfriend in the book."

I agreed 100%.

So what I did next was I went back to sleep, and it was a deep sleep. I woke briefly at 8.30am to text in sick (call centre, and I don't want to talk about it, thanks) then back into that deep, exhausted sleep I went. It was much like being in a cocooned chrysalis, and I can only assume I was gathering the strength I needed to fulfil this fictional man's desires.

I rose at around 4pm, nourished myself quickly on 6 hard boiled eggs, and then spent the evening ordering pens and notebooks online. By the next day I was ready.
I took a breath, and began creating a designated and healing writing space in my annex, which was complicated as I didn't have a desk or a chair. Anyway I took my mother's dressing table and wicker chair and covered them with tie dye cloths

and other sensory items, which are essential for me to work. I then took delivery of all my beautiful new stationary — and at last I was ready to write.

Since that first visitation there have been many others, and during each one I do my very best to listen and then when he's gone I translate his story into words pon page — for Chauncy does not communicate to me in human words, no no no. Rather he emits energetic vibrations. Yes, it's unorthodox but it works for us, so perhaps just accept it?

Suffice to say, Chauncy's plight has become my own plight as I endeavour to discover more about him and his life. Having that said I can switch off and do all my other creative bits and bobs when required and am also available for commissions, meetings with execs and so on. Give me a call!

Well, ideally look at my website where you'll find my contact details:
www.belladelarocher.com

Most of

A Novel

By Bella De La Rocher

[Notes to self in author's brackets]

CHAPTER 1

Chauncy Nathaniel Swanston, 33, good jaw line,
drives his car absentmindedly through the
streets of Doncaster and thinks about how he
really wants to avenge his parents' death.

He is thinking about it vigorously today
for… it is one year ago this very day since
his parents were murdered in their own home
while watching DIY SOS. [Send a copy of book
to Nick Knowles when finished?]

By the side of Chauncy sits his chiwawa,
Sadie [is she wearing a seatbelt? Decide
later]. Sadie is a canine capable of many
facial expressions using mainly her eyes. She
is also Chauncy's best friend and confidante,
and in many ways she is the closest he will
ever get to having a girlfriend.

[Actually I think Sadie can be in a specially
designed and manufactured car seat 'For
Dogs'.] [It was designed and manufactured by
Chauncy. By hand.] [Yes it passed all safety

regs etc etc.]

Like Chauncy, Sadie is also thinking
about how it was a year ago that Chauncy's
parents were murdered. 'Damn you, God!' she
thinks, looking up, then straight ahead, then
down, because she isn't sure she 100% believes
in god OR where he/she lives.

Chauncy holds the steering wheel with
the grip of an athlete, but tenderer.

Please note Chauncy is a very physically
striking man. His eyes, which are a piercing
green, are framed drastically by very black
eyelashes. Imagine the green eyes and black
eyelashes now. Then look up above the eyes and
you'll see he also has very black eyebrows,
and if you cast your eyes even further north
over the 7 or 8 inches of his forehead you'll
see he has white hair. Scan down his face now
to his excellent jaw line, and you're starting
to get the picture.

Chanucy runs a hand through his majestic
white hair and realises that without meaning
to, he has driven to his childhood home: the
house where his parents lived.

And died.

[good use of paragraphing]

His eyes fill with tears which make his

vision cloud up and go all foggy [metaphor].

Chauncy moved out of the family home and into his penthouse apartment which is in a converted mill a few years ago, before the killings, but the truth is that this house still means unfathomable things to him. He can vividly recall the happiness he and Sadie had here, with his mother and father, in this three-bed semi in the heart of the outskirts of Doncaster. The four of them were very relaxed in each others company and would oft [short for often] stay up late into the night doing bonding but clever things like playing scrabble. That was before they knew Chauncy's unborn twin was still in his mother's womb, so actually there were five of them.

CHAPTER 2

Chauncy parks up outside his dead parents'
house and looks at the front door, which is
red — as if the door its very self knew twould
be a house of spilt blood. If he had a penny
for every time he'd thought of painting the
red door white, like innocence, he'd be a
millionaire! He laughs like when people laugh
and cry at the same time and their eyes go all
sparkly. [Good]

"It's been a year now, Sadie my love,
and we are no closer to finding out whom
killed my parents! I have a feeling in my soul
that we must take up the murder investigation
ourselves. Sure, the police did what they
could, but they were limited and also ruled by
bigger powers, the kind of which no one could
comprehend. [For audio book / radio play
version the actor playing Chauncy should pause
here for about 3 seconds to allow listeners to
try to comprehend.] [They can't].

… We must go into this house,' Chauncy
continues saying, 'which I still own and have

the keys for, but which I have not set foot into for a whole year, and search for any clues which the police might have missed. BUT FIRST I think I'll go home to my penthouse apartment and have a quick shower." Chauncy says this suddenly, as if he wants to let warm water flow all over his naked body.

Sadie, knowing that Chauncy has a tendency to avoid his problems by over-washing, breathes out loudly through her nose.

3 HOURS LATER

Chauncy, his body soaped and rinsed, but still wet, steps out of his penthouse shower and onto plain lino i.e. not onto a mat [subtext: he is very body-confident] [possible sponsorship from DOVE if made into TV mini series?]

He DOES NOT put a towel on.

He looks into the bathroom mirror but he cannot see himself [symbolic] for it is steamed and blurry, like his feelings.

He decides to walk to his bedroom so he can have a look at himself in his full length mirror. As he makes this journey from one room to another he leaves wet footprints 'pon the carpet, but when he looks back at them - they have disappeared [brilliant]. This makes him think about how temporary and fleeting our time is on this Earth.

[OR: does he see another set of footprints by his side, because someone [probably Sadie] hath been accompanying him through his grief and loss??? Could become an important religious commentary book – this decade's *Da Vinci Code*?]

Before he gets to his full length mirror Chauncy just stands in his bedroom and looks around at all of his things. The colour scheme is grey, black and red. There is a rowing machine in the corner, and a globe of the world on a walnut desk. There is also a table with all of his favourite body sprays on it, and a walk-in wardrobe. The bed is really wide. When he bought the bed, the man at the Bed Showroom said it could comfortably fit eight females in it side by side and then he winked at him. Chauncy didn't take kindly to this and felt objectified on behalf of himself and all women.

He now walks over to his full length mirror and runs a hand through his wet white hair and thinks about having another shower.

Casting his mind back over the year since his parents' were killed, Chauncy acknowledges for the first time that he has gone through 23 soaps on a ropes.

Suddenly he shouts "Enough is enough!" commandingly, following that with this sentence: "It is as if I think I can scrub myself free of all the grief and loss and pain!"

Then he stands like a starfish on the balcony of his penthouse and lets whispers of wind dry his body.

Striding back into the apartment he wonders where Sadie is.

"Sadie, my love!" he calls, as he lunges nakedly through to the kitchen. He finds her perched on the kitchen island. This is where Chauncy does a lot of haute cuisine cooking [not for any women though].

"I am sorry, Sadie, for the way I have allowed myself to become dependent on having showers and baths and … I'm not afraid to admit it – the odd self-administered bed bath," [involves a flannel, bowl of water and fairy liquid] "But I am ready now, and we have much to do, Sadie. Somewhere out there is the killer whom killed my parents."

Sadie blinks in remembrance.

"Let us go now, back out into the metropolis of Doncaster again, back to my parents' house to find the clue that will lead us to the murderous fiends! And at the same time it would be nice if we can find their bodies so they can rest in peace and be reunited with their heads at last."

Sadie looks wistfully towards the freezer.

"Let us go now!" asserts Chauncy, still naked.

CHAPTER 3

"Oh but wait," says Chauncy, because he has noticed Sadie looking at the freezer. "Perhapenschance you are hungry, sweet child?"

Before Sadie can answer, Chauncy is striding towards the freezer with his hands on his hips and his skin still naked.

The thing is that Sadie was actually looking at the freezer because she was thinking about how the heads of Chauncy's parents are being stored in there. And anyway she is still full from lunch [what did she have? Something light, something that Jane Fonda might eat] but Chauncy is like a man on a mission, transfixed with the idea of cooking a meal for his beloved chiwawa.

Another avoidance technique, Sadie wonders? Yes.

Chauncy is now rummaging about in his chest freezer where, in amongst his and Sadie's food there are two human heads in two Sainsbury's carrier bags [one each][as in one carrier bag per head].

The orange of the Sainsbury's carrier bag is very useful, visually, so that Chauncy doesn't get his parents' heads mixed up with other large meat items, such as legs of lambs, shoulders of porks, and so on, when he is reaching in the freezer of a Saturday night to defrost something for him and Sadie's Sunday lunch. [Write a one-off theatrical farce where Chauncy accidentally defrosts his mum's head?]

"Nothing much in here, kiddo, just a couple of bags of hash browns and some onion rings. Oh and them heads. We could do with doing a big shop, really."

So he opens the fridge to have a look at what is in there. The fridge is very full of meat because Chauncy likes to eat a lot of it [meat].

"Hm," he says, thinking. "How about a couple of Steak Dianas?" he says this in a fatherly way, rubbing the top of Sadie's head with a tea towel.

Sadie moves away quickly and stares at him. She can't believe he's at it again: it's definitely another avoidance technique! *I'm not even hungry*, she tries to say with her eyes.

Chauncy is oblivious and decides to just

seize the moment and whiz up the Steak Dianes anyway. He reaches into the fridge and takes out two of his local butcher's locally sourced premium organic free range sirloin steaks. On the packet it says the name of the farmer whom delivered, raised, loved, and then slaughtered the meat.

Chauncy fries the steaks in several inches of butter and pours brandy on them before setting them on fire with a Bunsen Burner [check this is how you do Steak Dianes].

He then pops them onto two plates and garnishes with a bag of Pom Bears - Sadie's favourite, and sure to lure her out of her foul mood, which to be honest is really starting to dampen the mood of the first anniversary of his parents' death.

They sit opposite each other at the dining table and the atmosphere is tense. [When this is made into a film I want a bird's-eye view of the dining table, with Chauncy and Sadie at least 10 metres apart. This is called EXPRESSIONISM and it will show the emotional distance between them in this moment.]

Sadie's appetite is virtually non-existent but she manages a few mouthfuls of food, allowing a Pom Bear to dissolve slowly on her tongue. She does this while maintaining full eye contact with Chauncy. It is quite chilling.

Chauncy senses her tension and puts down his chopsticks.

"What's up with you? You've got a right face on," he says.

Sadie scoffs.

Chauncy regrets his tone. He sighs and holds his large head in his strong hands. "I'm sorry. I think I know what this is about. And you're right. I have been deliberately putting off going back into my parents' house to look for murder clues for some time now. First all the soapy showers and now I'm throwing myself into my cookery

[BOOK IDEA: A niche cookery book with lots of photos of Chauncy wearing an apron and cooking. Call it Chauncy's Chapattis? He's got all different aprons on. Sometimes it's just him in aprons nowhere near a cooker. Please note title also works with CHICKPEAS]

… What a fool I have been, Sadie! You of course have known this, haven't you? God you're intuitive. I know you've been trying to tell me to get my act together for so long now! Well Sadie I will not let you down any further, my girl – we're going now – out into the metropolis of Doncaster we will go – to solve this murder!"

A single tear falls from one of Sadie's eyes and splashes towards the plate of buttery charred meat in front of her. It lands on a Pom Bear and makes a hole in it, as if the tear itself were made of acid rain, a weather substance which was popular in the early 1990s.

Chauncy grabs one of his leather jackets and ties it around his waist. He then runs a finger down the CDs in his CD rack so he can choose what album they should listen to on the car journey. His finger stops on Phil Collins. 'Easy Lover' is a song which perfectly describes the one and only romantic relationship Chauncy has ever had, with a woman called Marianne: a step aerobics instructor with a heart of stone.

But then his eyes dart to his UB40 CD. It must be said that Chauncy is a fan of both world music and going on holidays and 'Red Red Wine' never fails to make him feel connected to the people of other cultures while also transporting him to sunnier climes. Should he listen to that to boost his morale?

Note bene (NB) : Neither song will affect his

driving, which is superb.

In the end he decides to go with 'Easy Lover' so he and Sadie can have a good sing-along and Chauncy can remind himself about how he doesn't ever want another girlfriend.

"Come on, girl — we've got a murder to solve!" he says as he grabs another leather jacket and hooks it on his finger and throws it over his shoulder. They exit the penthouse via the private lift which has a concierge waiting in it. "Ground floor, please, Godfrey," says Chauncy to Godfrey.

[When did Chauncy get dressed? Write that part later, in detail]

[Actually I want to do it now]

Chauncy did most of that cooking I just described while he was still in the nude after his shower, but when a window of opportunity presented itself, perhaps as the steaks were recovering from being Bunsened Burned, he nipped into his bedroom and opened his huge walk-in wardrobe with both hands, and said "Ta da!". Why? Because that's just something he always does whenever he opens his wardrobe.

"*What to wear, what to wear…*" he pondered. The thing about Chauncy is that his body is very instinctual and actually it has its own ideas about fashion. So he cleared his mind, closed his eyes, put his hands in front of him and ran a finger along the rail. When he opened them he was holding a tight black sleeveless polo neck and a pair of tight pale grey leather trousers. "What body wants, body gets," said Chauncy, grabbing his peach moccasins to finish the look.

He then covered himself in talcum powder and slipped leg after leg [but just two legs] into the legs of the leather trousers. Then he walked past his full length mirror, while looking at himself discreetly as if he was a passerby looking at himself. Then he stopped, back-tracked to the mirror and said, "Oh hi! I didn't expect to see you. Yes, I'm very well, thank you, and you? Yes, a lot of people say I look like Ross Poldark. But with white hair. Well actually I'm just on my way to my dead parents' house to look for clues about their murder which happened a year ago today."

A silence befalls the conversation, because the other person doesn't know what to say about that because they are emotionally stunted.

Anyway Chauncy has had enough of this pretend conversation with the passerby who is actually him, and he's feeling a bit confused.

It's time to get back to the steak! So he does
that and then the things happen that I've
already written such as the groundbreaking
tender scene of him and Sadie and the Pom
Bears where Chauncy realises he's been having
too many baths etc and now we're up to the
part where they've exited the penthouse via
the private elevator.

CHAPTER 4

Chauncy and Sadie exit the penthouse via the private elevator and Chauncy gives Godfrey, the private elevator operator, twenty pounds. "Gawd bless ya," Godfrey says.

They are now in the underground garage, where Chauncy carefully buckles Sadie into her bespoke dog seat in the passenger side of his car [it's a Rolls Royce].

He then closes the car door and stands there for a minute with one hand on top of the car and the other over his face. He takes a deep breath through his long artistic fingers and says *Come on come on come on* to himself over and over and over. What he is doing here is getting himself ready to go and look for clues in his dead parents' house about whom killed them.

[I can't help but wonder what Chauncy has been doing this past year, apart from having showers? Could write a prequel?]

He walks around to the driver's door and

opens it and puts one leg into the car and then bends down and moves sideways so his bum is on the seat and then he pulls his other leg in. He is now in the car. [Too much detail?] [No]

He opens the flap above the window [check technical term later] and looks in the little mirror at himself. His eyes, which if you recall are green and surrounded by thick black eye lashes with black eyebrows above them, are sparkling like the debris in the tail-end of a shooting star. [Woosh!]

His white hair, which has just dried quite naturally into a quiff after his long soapy shower, looks great. He blinks quickly to try and get a look at what he looks like with his eyes closed. "IMPOSSIBLE!" he concludes, before closing the flap again.

Sadie has just been sitting there all this time. "So patient, you are, Sadie," he says, tapping the top of her head with a biro from the glove compartment.

"Let's fire up this automobile and get going! And I've decided we'll listen to 'Easy Lover' by Phil Collins on repeat for the whole 20 minute drive. I am going to use the time to remind myself about my failed relationship with that BACKSTABBER Marianne just to keep the memory fresh so I don't get distracted by another woman ever again."

Sadie isn't sure this is the healthiest attitude to take, even though she wasn't Marianne's biggest fan. Marianne once placed Sadie in the tie back of a curtain for safe-keeping while she did the hoovering, which was considerate of her on the one hand but ultimately not very dignified for Sadie.

Chauncy revs up the engine and puts his feet on all the right pedals of the car and hits 'Play' on the state of the art stereo system. 'Easy Lover' begins with its drum beat and what sounds someone playing a small Yamaha keyboard. Both Chauncy and Sadie nod their heads with the beat. They also both scoff at this line:

"She will play around and leave you.

Leave you and deceive you"

"Ha!" laughs Chauncy, knowingly. "Well she certainly did that…"

THIS IS A FLASHBACK

Chauncy casts his mind back to the first time he saw Marianne, his one and only ever girlfriend. She was his step aerobics instructor and it was summer 1999. What a summer!

He was new to the sport and she stole his heart and made it pump faster than it ever had before. Up and down on the step he went, sometimes lifting small hand-weights at the same time, every Tuesday night at the leisure centre 7pm – 8pm.

With each passing week he became more confident, placing his step closer to the front of the class, sometimes even allowing himself to lock eyes with Marianne, the lycra-covered temptress.

He was only 18, while she was in her 30s yet looked more like mid-40s. She watched him transform from a shy, awkward exerciser into a master of the step, a virtuoso who never missed a beat, as he became more toned and nimble as the weeks went on.

One night, at the end of the class, Chauncy pretended to be having trouble with the zip of his bumbag but really he was just waiting for everyone else to leave the sports hall so at last he could speak to Marianne, for some reason. This was made difficult because one of the older women, Sandra, was dawdling around Chauncy, asking if she and her husband Keith who had come to pick her up could touch his calfs and so on. He allowed

them one quick brush each just to get rid of
them.

Once they were out of the way, Chauncy
gathered himself together, distributed all his
energy equally into all his chakras, and then
lurched across the hall to where Marianne was
trying to style her frizzy post-workout hair
[waste of time]. At last they were alone!

"Where did you get your cycling shorts
from?" Chauncy asked.

"Bon Marché," Marianne replied. He was
shocked but he tried not to show it. Looking
back it was obvious, but he was young, naïve.
And didn't she know it! She moved towards him,
as if she was about to kiss him.

BUT THEN she quickly moved away and
sauntered over to her ghetto blaster. Chauncy
gulped. He'd never been kissed before and he
was nervous. It was all well and good stepping
onto and off of a box with supreme rhythm but
here, in the quiet of the deserted sports
hall, he was scared.

Marianne looked through her box of
cassettes. She selected one and put it in the
machine. Then she fast forwarded and rewound
it for a bit until she found the track she was
looking for.

It was 'Mambo No 5', the hit of the

summer. She danced back over to Chauncy, clapping her hands to the song's undeniable beat. When she got to him she took hold of his large head and pulled his face to hers.

Then she kissed him while dancing on the spot, which made the experience a jolty one. It was actually quite like kissing someone while they were doing step aerobics. He guessed she just couldn't switch off.

She didn't stop kissing him for the whole song.

When it finished she pulled back and shouted jubilantly, "You make me feel like Geri Halliwell!" before unplugging her ghetto blaster and running out of the hall with it.

Chauncy was both elated and deflated – and so many questions ran through his mind. Was she is his girlfriend now? What would happen next week? Bon Marché — really?

Well, the following week the same thing happened, and the week after that. Chauncy hung about at the end of every class and each time Marianne chose a different song to kiss him to, and it was always something up-tempo. Shania Twain, Cher, Ricky Martin and so on.

It was a fairly magical time and they soon moved in together, with Sadie as well [this was before Chauncy got the Penthouse] [so it was just a basic flat, probably above a shop] and they were happy. Well, actually he wouldn't go that far. He was content in a way that people who don't know any better often are. Until…

Until ONE NIGHT when Chauncy went to pick Marianne up from work as a surprise. He had ceased being a participant in her step aerobics class — that was Marianne's idea — she said now they were an item it would be unethical and she would be in breach of the hypocratic oath.

Chauncy went into the leisure centre to locate her class. He could hear music. He started to move with the beat, as if it was speaking to a deep part of his memory.

It was Mambo No 5.

He danced his way to the door of the sports hall. Suddenly he knew what he would find if he opened that door. He opened the door. And he was right. There she was, kissing a young man who wasn't him, to the mambo trumpet beat.

BACK TO THE PRESENT DAY

A single tear rolls down Chauncy's cheek but it dries very quickly because he's already feeling better.

"I'm glad I remembered about all that anyway Sadie because it's a good reminder that I don't need anyone else in my life. Right then let's get on with this, we're nearly at my parents' house now. I'll turn Phil Collins off."

Sadie enjoys the sound of nothing in her large ears.

They pull up outside the house and Sadie thinks how this is how the day started, 3 chapters ago now.

Oftentimes, on Chauncy's lips is the ghost of a smile. This is not one of those times. He is in absolute hell whilst at the same time feeling very brave. He takes a deep breath in and blows it out again.

"Come on Sadie," he says, "Let us go now into the house. It will be difficult for us, yes, but what we must remember is that this was a house of happiness before it was a house of horror and macabre things. We must remember and call upon the love we felt here for your Grandma and Grandpa Swanston and let it carry us into the garden and through the front door."

They both take a deep breath and get out of the car, closing the doors behind them.

Then Chauncy locks the car, and then they walk to the garden gate, where they stop and take some more deep breaths. Chauncy puts a hand on the gate and pauses for this is a monumental moment.

[When this is made into a film I want a close up on Chauncy's pale hand holding the gate, and then the camera pans down to Sadie's paw which is also touching the gate but lower down, then back up to Chauncy's hand but the camera turns a bit and travels up his leg to get there. The only sound to accompany these shots MUST be Chauncy's heart beat.]

Then Chauncy whispers, "It is time" and together they push open the gate, which doesn't creek.

CHAPTER 5

As they walk down the garden path, both Chauncy and Sadie look at the flowerbeds either side of the path, noticing that they are very well kept.

"What the…" says Chauncy. "Who has been keeping the garden nice? It should be overgrown! No one hath lived here for a year! I expected a mess! Weeds, dead flowers, rats living here and there – that's what I imagined! Yet look – tis as if a green fingered fairy hast been taking care of it!"

Just then a man with the same physical body and face as Chauncy steps out from behind a bush. He is wearing galoshes and gardening gloves but there is no mistaking the fact that he LOOKS ALMOST EXACTLY LIKE CHAUNCY.

Chauncy gasps. "Who are you???" he enquires, face to face with what can only be described as hot perfection.

The man before him is almost his exact double - apart from instead of black eyebrows and white head hair he has the opposite: white

eyebrows and black head hair. [Very striking.]
[Film poster idea: the two Chauncies side by
side staring intently into camera] [OR at each
other] [OR back to back]

"Who… are… you?" asks Chauncy.

"Chauncy Nathaniel Swanston," replies
the other Chauncy.

"But that's… my name," says Chauncy.

The new Chauncy appears to have not
heard him. He has bent down to stroke a plant
like it is a pet.

"How did… you… get here?" asks Chauncy,
confusedly.

"This is my parents' house," replies
Chauncy.

"But… it's MY parents' house, and they
are dead…" says Chauncy.

"No they're not, they're in the living
room watching Downton Abbey," says Chauncy.

Chauncy stares towards the living room
window. He knows Chauncy can't be right - his
parents hated Downton Abbey, they saw it as an
indulgent celebration of an outmoded class
system. Also he has their heads at home in his
freezer.

He casts his mind back to a moment ago

when this Chauncy first appeared. He seemed to come out of nowhere, simply stepping out from behind a bush.

Chauncy has a walk over to the bush and looks around the back of it. It is there where he sees where this Chauncy must have come from: for there is a rip in the fabric of space and time! The other Chauncy must have slipped through it from a parallel universe.

Chauncy looks at Chauncy. He looks very serene. When he takes his gardening gloves off to wipe his brow, Chauncy notices he is wearing a wedding ring. What a privileged life he must lead in his parallel universe! Why hath HE, this Chauncy, in this world, been the one to feel pain and loss and heartbreak? Why doth HE, the other Chauncy, have all the luck?

A rage builds up in Chauncy. He feels all of his toned body tense up. The tension starts in his strong shoulders and goes all the way around to his dynamic chest, where it explores slowly down, down, down his torso, quietly to his groin, then it hurries around to his buttocks, then back round the front again, then keeps going south down his wide thighs to his knees, then it goes back up again for a minute but then sweeps down and rests on his bulbous calves.

But then the other Chauncy smiles at him and it is like all of the stars in the night sky are shining from his face. It dissolves all of Chauncy's tension and all of his bodily muscles relax.

In fact, he feels very jubilant – how lucky he is to have met his self from another world! He has always wanted a brother or sister and it is especially nice to have one which is not an unborn twin in his mother's womb. He imagines all the things they can do together.

"Do you have any pets?" Chauncy asks.

"Yes, I have a chiwawa," he says.

"Me too! She is called Sadie. Wait a minute, where IS Sadie? She was just here a minute ago when I went around to have a look behind that bush… Oh no — she must have slipped though the fabric of space and time into YOUR world!" Chauncy aghasts. "I must go into YOUR world to find her!" he says to the other Chauncy. The other Chauncy has gone back to stroking plants like pets.

"Can you help me?" Chauncy asks. "Can you be my guide into the other realm from whence you came? So I can get my chiwawa?"

The other Chauncy just looks at him blankly.

"You know, back into that rip in space and time to your garden. I appreciate all the care you are bestowing into my garden but you do realise you've travelled to another universe, don't you?"

The other Chauncy keeps looking at him blankly.

Chauncy sighs. He needs to work quickly to convince this other Chauncy that this is not his home, and that he has slipped through a portal, so they can both bob back through it.

"Look," says Chauncy to Chauncy, "I don't think you understand what's happening here. This," he pauses, gestures around him, "this is not… …your world."

Nothing.

"Don't you think this is a little odd? That there's another version of you in front of you? And that's me: an identical tall, toned, striking man with an excellent jawline and the ability to look good in anything, even a bin bag?"

"I wore a bin bag once…"

"Hallo'we'en 1991," they say at the same time.

The other Chauncy gasps.

Chauncy continues: "School disco. You were 10 years old. All the other kids had bin bags on as well, but theirs were hanging loose. You used a system of belts and sellotape to create a more stylish fit. And you teamed the ensemble with a…"

"…raspberry beret."

"Exactly."

"You mean? You wore… the same… outfit at your Halloween school disco?"

"Yes - but I was here, in this universe. You're from another one, one where you're married, where your parents aren't dead. I guess we have both experienced some of the same things, and yet… some things are very… different." Chauncy looks away. [excellent]

The other Chauncy stares at the house. "So, my, your - parents, they're not, in there, watching Downton?"

Chauncy shakes his head. "No." He thinks about telling Chauncy all the details about their murder but he knows it wouldn't do any good.

"No," he continues, "your parents aren't in this house — but they're in the one in your world. And we need to go there," he points - "through that rip in the fabric of space and time, can you see it? Just to the right of that bush. It's how you got here."

"Oh I see! Come on then," the other Chauncy says [finally].

CHAPTER 6

Both the Chauncies walk to the bush. Chauncy takes the opportunity to have a good look at Chauncy. It's quite a treat to see himself in 3D. He hangs back and watches himself walk ahead for a few steps. Lovely.

They stop at the bush. Our Chauncy asks Chauncy a question. "How did it feel? On your way through the portal?"

"Well I didn't even know I'd gone anywhere did I, so it should all be quite straightforward."

"True. Come on then. We should probably hold hands so we don't lose each other. Can you imagine if we ended up in the wrong universe! Nightmare." [Spin off idea]

The Chauncies hold hands and walk towards the rip. As they get right up to it it shines like a curtain made of a million diamonds and when Chauncy pulls the curtain back it is like looking at a newly born star. How did the other Chauncy not notice this on his way through? He looks at him and you can tell it's not really registering again.

Suddenly the brilliant light opens up and a force pulls them forward like nothing Chauncy has ever felt before, apart from when he's accidentally caught himself on the Dyson hoover pipe.

Then BAM! They are in the parallel universe, in the other Chauncy's front garden. The other Chauncy looks at the flowerbeds and says "I thought I'd weeded these already…"

Chauncy sighs. He isn't sure he can keep explaining to Chauncy what's going on. The important thing is he's returned him back to his own world and now it's time to locate Sadie.

"Sadie my love!" he calls. She does not come. Perhaps she has gone round to the back garden, he suggests to himself. Walking around the side of the house he realises he can hear her - she's doing that little happy noise she makes when she's with another dog - a kind of snore crossed with a laugh crossed with chest pains.

As he enters the back garden he is faced with a scene which is both beautiful and unbearable: because of course! In this universe his parents are alive and their heads are on top of their bodies.

His mother is picking blackberries and wearing a sunhat.

His father is watering the garden with a hose pipe and every so often he jokingly douses Chauncy's mother. She scolds him in that way that people do when actually they love what is happening and feel very connected to each other.

Sadie is trotting around with the other Sadie, the happiest he hath seen her in years.

None have noticed this Chauncy yet.

And there is a younger woman, it must be the other Chauncy's wife, doing some lunges. She has long black frizzy hair and the figure of someone who leads a step aerobics class 3-4 nights a week.

She turns. It is Marianne! "Chauncy! Darling!" she shouts to him. The other Chauncy, her real husband, is still in the front garden, tending those flowerbeds he is obsessed with.

It seems that Marianne thinks our Chauncy is her Chauncy — and she isn't alone in that. His mother and father do as well. They all walk towards him. His mother holds out her arms. Chauncy fills with emotions.

"Look at you! Your hair and eyebrows have swapped round in terms of their colour. And you look more intelligent. Are you ok?" she asks.

Just then Sadie stops her trotting around the garden with the other chiwawa and looks at him. She knows. She knows this is not his world, or hers. But she looks so happy. And Chauncy could be happy here too. Couldn't he…?

Marianne strides towards him, as clad in Bon Marché lycra as she ever was. There might even be a touch of BHS in her style. They mustn't have gone into administration in this universe then. I wonder how the high street in general is doing, in this world? Chauncy ponders.

[TV SHOW IDEA: Just something where Chauncy is walking around high streets talking to the camera about rising rent prices etc then popping into shops and looking understanding then trying a few outfits on] And is Marianne a cowbag in this universe as well, Chauncy wonders? [PROBABLY]

His parallel parents are standing in front of him, smiling and saying things like "Are you all right?" and they are saying that because Chauncy has gone very verbally quiet.

What is happening here is there are thoughts running around in his head and emotions catapulting up and down his trunk and limbs because he is looking at his parents' alive faces for the first time in over a year.

His mother walks over to him and rests a large hand on his forearm.

"Chauncy? Shall we go inside and do a wordsearch? Or if you like you can show me how many skips you can do on the skipping rope?"

Oh how he would love to say yes! He feels like a young boy again.

Then he realises that he hasn't done a wordsearch or shown off with a skipping rope for quite some years, so the fact she's suggesting it means it must be the kind of thing the other Chauncy still does. Which makes sense.

But he must admit there is something appealing about the offer. His father is walking towards him with a skipping rope. "Here you go, my boy! Have a skip!" He is saying this joyfully and laughing with his mouth and eyes open quite wide.

Chauncy takes the skipping rope. Everyone stands around him

[For the TV/Film version: this MUST be shot from Chauncy's POV - everyone's laughing faces and mouths are saying "Skip! Skip! Skip!" and they are clapping - but out of time and out of focus - this is a metaphor for Chauncy's current state and feelings].

Even Sadie and the other Sadie have joined in!

He doesn't know what to do. On the one hand he's having a good time but on the other it feels a bit like being mugged. He holds the rope like he is going to start skipping

- but then quite very SUDDENLY -

Sadie jumps up onto his shoulder and makes a little truffle sound in his ear. He instantaneously understands *exactly* what she is trying to communicate. It is this:

"Stop now, for we don't belong here, it's all a bit weird actually and that other chiwawa isn't right in the head, all she does is trot around the garden looking for moths to eat, and I had to stop her from rummaging in the bins a couple of times. Sorry I know it's my fault we're here because I slipped through the portal, thanks for coming to get me, and I know you must want to kill the other Chauncy so we can stay here in his place but we mustn't, it would be like living a lie, and it

wouldn't be long before SHE hurts you again,"
Sadie gives Marianne a sly look. "Oh and also
what about whomever killed your parents, in
our world? We should crack on trying to solve
that, really."

Chauncy 100% agrees with her.

He barges past the circling chanting
crowd, and, with Sadie still on his shoulder,
he strides towards the front garden. Before he
gets there he stops and puts Sadie down, then
he leans his forehead on the house, pushing
his head onto the bricks while making a noise
like crying being held inside of a mountain.

"It is difficult to leave but I know I
must!" he splutters, then he gets himself
together and walks to the front garden where
the rip in the fabric of space and time is
located.

The other Chauncy is still weeding his
beloved flowerbeds, but he looks up when he
senses Chauncy and Sadie standing next to him.

"We're leaving. It wouldn't be right if
we were to… stay," says Chauncy to Chauncy.

"Okey-dokey then, well I was just going
to have a break and ask Mum to watch me doing
some skipping anyway. Well it's been nice,
have a good journey back, see ya," he

chirrups.

That could have been me, Chauncy thinks, *showboating with a skipping rope while the delighted and petrifying faces of my parents stared at me.*

"Yet it is not to be", he whispers as a single tear falls from his left tear duct.

The other Chauncy stands up and peels his t-shirt off, he then steps forward and uses it to wipe this Chauncy's tears. Then they look at each other for a moment longer than is natural.

Sadie gasps.

Then they both turn away.

Sadie exhales.

The other Chauncy says, "Bon Voyage" but without a French accent, then he walks away to the back garden, to his wife and parents and slow chiwawa. Chauncy and Sadie watch him go.

"Ready, my girl?" says Chauncy.

Sadie nods.

He picks her up and they bob back through the rip in time and space and before they know it they are back in their own front garden. They do not make any efforts to seal the portal.

"Right let's get on with solving this murder," Chauncy says, for what feels like the hundredth time.

CHAPTER 7

Chauncy takes his house keys out of the pocket of his leather jacket which is still tied around his waist and puts his hand on the front door handle, and when he does this all kinds of memories of previous times he's opened this door flash through his mind's eye.

All of a sudden he feels 16 again, coming home after a day of army training [self-taught] or working in the local charity shop, or running around the neighbourhood as fast as he could. But now isn't the time to be reminiscing! It is time to open the door, and to start piecing together the clues that will lead him to his parents' murderer.

Chauncy uses his gallant hand to open the door and into his dead parents' house they go.

He steps over the step, stepping onto the hallway carpet which is green and woolly. Feeling the buoyancy of it underfoot, he says, "Some things never change", and smiles to himself. Sadie's feet sink into the deep shag.

It comes up to her knees.

Everything is as twas whence they were last here except for one thing: an intense and purifying smell of decay! Suddenly Chauncy worries that the heads of his parents have defrosted in the freezer but then he remembers he moved them to the chest freezer in his penthouse apartment last year, so no worries.

"Phew!" He rasps. Then he walks into the kitchen and sees the source of the decay: flowers, there are dead flowers everywhere! Hundreds of dead flowers.

"What sorcery is this?!" exclaims Chauncy, as the smell of rotting flower flesh gets right up and inside his and Sadie's noses. The stench determinedly hangs onto their tiny nostril hairs like … [think of metaphor later.] [Also check if dogs have nostril hair.]

What is happening here is a putrid smell is coming from a mound of dead flowers which are all piled up by the back door.

"But how did they… get… in here?" enquires Chauncy. He strides forwards and uses his long arms and large hands like spades, bashing the flowers out of the way to reveal…

"Sadie's dog flap! It has been unlocked this entire year?! And someone hath been pushing bunches of flowers through it?!"

Being back in his murdered parents' home is difficult enough, but what is the meaning of this? Whom would play with him in such a manner? He feels like an action man doll in a terrible puppet show where the other puppets are a lot bigger than him and he's been made to wear an outfit he doesn't really like [he still looks great].

He leans with his back against the stainless steel fridge and freezer [one of those with an ice cube dispenser — Peter Andre's got one] then he slides down it until he is resting on his haunches [possible spin-off TV show: 'Chauncy's Haunches' - scenes of Chauncy on his haunches in various exotic locations.] [Might work better as a calendar?]

He runs a hand through his white quiff. Then he licks his index fingers and smooths his black eyebrows down with saliva. He then turns around and looks at his blurry reflection in the stainless steel fridge. Looking good. He moves forward so his actual nose touches his mirrored nose, then he dips his head to one side and pouts. His lips touch his mirrored lips. Lovely. [He really could play Ross Poldark.]

Chauncy shakes himself out of his simmering moment with himself up against the fridge, and turns back round to the decomposing flowers. *I would look good on horseback on top of a Cornish cliff,* he thinks.

"I came back here to find clues about whom killed my parents, not to find someone has posted dozens of bunches of flowers through my dog's doorway!" he bellows.

Sadie has been quite quiet these past few minutes. Suddenly he notices it is because she is truffling around in the dead flowers. Every so often she picks something up in her teeth and drops it at his side.

"Sadie... what are you... doing?" asks Chauncy.

He inspects the pile she hath created. It is a pile of cards! Each putrid bunch of flowers must have come with a card – and Sadie is locating them all! *What an intellect she is,* Chauncy thinks. He also thinks, and not for the first time, that she is the single most important female in his life.

He leaps up from his hindquarters and plants a firm kiss on the back of his own hand then stamps the memory of it onto Sadie's head. Then he looks through the cards she has collected. There are 21 of them. Each card has a different letter of the alphabet written on it.

The letters are:

S E A H O M A R E S E I J L N B I R D E R

and there is also an item of punctuation, it is a comma: ,

"Right then Sadie I think what we have here is a message from the person whom killed my parents. We need to decode what the message is. Shall we have a sit down at the dining table and see what we can come up with? We could have a glass of port, maybe lay on a few nibbles, make an event of it?"

Sadie sighs.

"OK I get the picture," Chauncy replies, tapping the top of Sadie's head with a dead flower.

CHAPTER 8

They sit at the dining table and get straight
to the task in hand, laying the cards out in
front of them. Chauncy is holding a Parker Pen
in his left hand, for he is left handed, like
a lot of the world's most interesting people
are.

"Well I say we keep rearranging the
letters until we see the message," says
Chauncy. This is exactly what Sadie had in
mind.

Once again the letters are:
S E A H O M A R E S E I J L N B I R D E R

They begin moving them around, like they're
having a game of Boggle. After about an hour
they have found some good words such as:

SEA

HOME

MARE

BIRD

and [and is not one of the words]

RED

"But none of this means anything!" rages
Chauncy.

Oh dear, thinks Sadie, this isn't doing
any good. She perceives that they both need a
break. She leaps down from the table and trots
out into the back garden to do some ancient
breathing techniques, which she knows how to
do instinctively.

Chauncy follows her onto the patio and
stands behind her, listening to her breath. It
sounds like she's got asthma, he thinks.

"Hey kid, it sounds like you've got
asthma," he says. Sadie ignores him because
her mind is currently floating on a lake.

The truth is, Chauncy is also quite
enlightened. He thinks about the time he spent
in a monastery in the South of France doing
meditations and martial arts. [Would make a
really good montage sequence]

I guess I've just… disconnected from all
of that, he suggests to himself, adding:
Because of the traumatic year I have been
through.

"The monks... in the monastery... they taught me a technique for mind focus. Perhaps I should try it now. It sounds perfect for this situation doesn't it, Sadie? It should help me to see the message from the letters on the cards. But it involves me getting into a bit of a rabid state so you had better stand back."

He begins by closing his eyes and breathing in and out very deeply. Faster and faster he goes, in and out, until he is panting hard, so hard. Then he starts to sweat furiously and beads of sweat fall from his forehead and drop down his body. He licks his salty upper lip and gasps while looking up at the sky, then he finds his top has stuck to him, and has gone quite see-through, and his pale grey leather trousers are clinging to his strong thighs

– and then very SUDDENLY –

he runs at full speed back into the house. It has worked — he has focused his mind and can now solve the puzzle!

Sadie follows him and watches how quickly he works, it's like he is being fast-forwarded, moving the letters around to

decipher the hidden anagrammatical message,
getting closer to the killer's communication
each time.

These are some of the things he comes up with:

ER, JEANS BILE MOHAIR DRES

JEANER, DRESSHAIR MOBILE

DRESS JEAN, REHAIR MOBILE

Until finally he hits upon this:

JEAN, MOBILE HAIRDRESSER

Chauncy immediately snaps out of his trance.

"My mother's mobile hairdresser was
called Jean! SHE is the murderer!"

Sadie gasps.

Just then there is a noise near the back
door. Chauncy and Sadie hurtle to the kitchen
to see the dog flap is flapping!

"What in the hell…?!!" verbalises
Chauncy as he watches what can only be
described as a grown woman trying to push
herself through the dog flap into his dead

parents' kitchen.

It's Jean, the mobile hairdresser whom I have just told you about! Chauncy remembers her from his time living here because she used to come round every Thursday morning to give his mother's hair a wash and set. Also, every other Thursday his father would allow Jean to lightly trim his hair – taking an agreed maximum deduction of 2mm from the length.

Chauncy's father had jet black hair and was very protective of it, and rightly so.

"Isn't it funny how your father hasn't got one grey hair and yet you Chauncy, a man half his age, have hair the colour of Colgate toothpaste?" Jean would say.

At the time Chauncy didn't think much of it, but looking at her now, squirming through an animal's entrance and / or exit, he is filled with fury.

He strides over to her wriggling body. So far she has just got her head through the flap and it is facing upwards, looking at him.

"What are you doing here???" he demands, placing a foot onto her forehead. "Is it you whom has sent all these flowers? Or is it someone else whom knows it is YOU whom killed my parents???" He continues.

"Can you take your foot off my head a

minute?" asks Jean.

Chauncy sighs and lifts his peach moccasin from her forehead. He's not a monster.

"Ok but start talking scissor hands or it won't be such a soft shoe next time!"

Jean gulps. She knows she's on borrowed time.

"Chauncy… it… it wasn't me! I didn't kill your parents! I've been set up! I didn't deliver the flowers either, whomever did has framed me!"

Chauncy eyes her suspiciously.

"Then what EXACTLY are you doing here?"

Jean begins wriggling again, desperate to finish her journey through the dog flap.

"Jean, I don't think you're going to fit through there if I'm honest," Chauncy advises. "This dog flap was commissioned for a chiwawa."

"You might be right. If I reverse back outside will you let me in through the door?"

"Yes, certainly."

Jean shimmies back through the flap into the garden.

CHAPTER 9

Chauncy decides to take a moment to rehydrate himself. He brings his lips to the kitchen tap and drinks directly from it, like an American person.

Then he struts across the kitchen to the backdoor. Through the frosted glass he can see the outline of Jean, waiting to be let in. Just as he turns the key and opens the door he hears the unmistakable sound of dog's hoof running on lino: Sadie - and she's by his side with a bulb of garlic.

"Sadie, what are you…?"

BUT HE CANNOT FINISH HIS SENTENCE BECAUSE

Jean, Chauncy's dead parents' mobile hairdresser, has pushed her way through the open door and into the kitchen and revealed her true self: Jean is a vampire!!!

She is in the kitchen wearing a black cape with red lining and the collar sticking up, and she also has fangs, very pale skin, and a bouffant haircut.

"Jean… what the heck is going on?" commands Chauncy.

"Do not be afraid, for I mean you no harm," Jean purrs, taking in the sight of him, visually, then stepping towards him and licking her lips.

Chauncy reverses backwards, worried she is going to make moves on him. He knows full well he'd make a breath-takingly physically outstanding vampyre [spell it like that from now on] but he's just not ready for that kind of commitment.

How to distract her? He wonders. Meat! He reaches into the fridge and throws a steak [how long has that been in there?] towards the back door with the idea being that Jean will scamper after it and he can then shove her back out of the door. As he does this, Jean merely throws her head back and laughs.

"Oh my boy, you know very little about the true nature of being vampyre!" As she laughs her fangs are really prominent and it makes Chauncy gulp down a lot of air in dread.

Jean lifts up from the ground and hovers then glides across the kitchen towards him.

"No! No! Jean! No Jean! No!" cries Chauncy.

He quickly fumbles in his bumbag in which he always keeps a penknife, some string, and lots of loose nails [from his time in the SAS].

Jean looks at the bumbag. She seems to know exactly what he's thinking. Then her gaze moves from the bumbag and onto Chauncy's thighs, before flicking up to his face and locking onto his eyes with her eyes. Chauncy finds he cannot move, he has been immobilised! He looks like a Greek statue, but more chiseled.

Jean begins chanting the most beautiful sounds, like this: "Ah-ah-ah-ah-ah", up and down the scales: low to high to low, staying low, back to high, high, high, LOW, low, HIIIIIGH, and Chauncy is powerless and hypnotised by it.

Sadie is watching the scene unfold, the garlic bulb still at her feet.

And it is quite a sight: a grown man with one hand in his bumbag, his mouth agape [but jawline still very defined], eyes sparkling like two crystal gemstones, staring at a floating 60-something vampyre who is singing like a preteen all-male choir [was

Chauncy ever in a choir?].

Just what is going on in Chauncy's mind's eye? Sadie ponders.

CUT TO: Chauncy's mind's eye

Something incredibly supernatural is happening: Jean is providing Chauncy with a direct link to his dead parents! She is allowing him to see their final moments!

It is a wonderful scene: they are both sitting in their armchairs watching DIY SOS, dipping custard creams into cups of tea. His mother's hair looks nice, with it being a Thursday Jean has been round earlier and given it a wash and set. Every so often she touches it and smiles and pouts to herself at the same time. Chauncy wonders if that actually happened or if Jean is manipulating this scene to make her hairdressing look more appreciated. He can't tell. Then his father looks at his mother [as in Chauncy's mother, not his own mother] and reaches out to touch her arm, he does this for no other reason than that he loves her. It really is a moving slice of their lives.

BUT THEN SUDDENLY

there is a knock at the door [still in the past] It must be the murderer! But his parents do not know that! Chauncy says "Nooooooooooo dooooooooooon't aaaaaaaaaaannnswwwwer iiiiiiiiiiit" but they can't hear him – his father gets up and walks to the hallway – and at this crucial point, which would provide vitally important clues about whom killed his parents, Chauncy snaps out of the trance-spell he has been under.

His head feels like he has eaten two ice lollies, quickly. He holds the sides of his head with the flat of his palms.

Jean is now making a noise like a rabbit eating a carrot. Her head is going mad, jerking around.

He strides over to her, grabs her shoulders and gives her a good shake. "Just what is going on?" Chauncy requests commandingly.

Jean opens her mouth to answer and a wasp flies out.

Then she goes completely limp and dies. Chauncy drops her on the ground, and as she hits the granite-tiled floor she shatters like pottery.

"That's that then," Chauncy concludes, opening the back door to let the wasp out.

He looks at Sadie and says, "Back to square one, then kiddo. Maybe what I will do is have a think back to what I was doing on the night my parents were killed in case I have missed any vital clues."

Sadie lets out a long sigh.

CHAPTER 10

THIS IS A FLASHBACK

TO EXACTLY ONE YEAR AGO

So just where was Chauncy when his parents were being killed? He was having a night out at the Casino, a place where he fitted in in a glamorous, and not seedy, way. He likes to play Black Jack the best.

Chauncy doesn't go to the casino often, but when he does he goes alone [he takes Sadie of course] and when he's there he gets on really well with all the other men and doesn't take any notice of the women. Even though the women really really try to get his attention, he will just not look at them at all except by accident.

He was doing one of his accidental looks around the room on this occasion when he saw someone he recognized from his long ago past: Marianne. *Ugh, her,* he thought, *and what IS she wearing?* [Answer: an ill-fitting emerald green dress which was too tight under the arms.]

Anyway seeing her made his blood run like hot oil in a chip pan: fizzy, dangerous, unhealthy. [If Chauncy ever has a heart attack it will be her fault.]

He shook his head violently as if he could shake her image away from his vision. Then he decided to check if one of the coupiers [is that the word?] could also see her, in case he was having a day terror.

"Hey man, do me a favour will ya, look over there, next to the 2p machines, can you see a lady? Over there, in the emerald green halter neck dress which would look nice with a teal cardigan over it, over there? Can you see that woman? Tell me, man, can you?!"

The coupier looked startled by Chauncy's sudden anger, but because he was a regular he knew him and respected him and therefore he was more worried <u>for</u> him than <u>of</u> him. The coupier opened his mouth to answer Chauncy's question but at that very moment an alarm went off, a very loud alarm which made all the security men put their radios to their ears and look afraid but in a prepared way.

What was happening? Was it about to be a Code Red situation? Yes. Very quickly anarchy erupted, the loud alarm blaring out had made everyone go absolutely feral: some were eating their plastic tokens, one man was trying to carry a slot machine out, and there were peanuts all over the floor.

Because of his time as the only ever British person to be allowed to be a US Navy Seal, Chauncy knew exactly how to deal with a high octane situation like this. He kept a cool head and a laser-focus, and anyway he had the safety of only one person on his mind: Sadie. He'd dropped her off in the casino's Dog Lounge upon arrival, so he ran in that direction through the chaotic mayhem.

Oh how now, with hindsight; a year later, he wishes he had left Sadie at home that night; for perhaps she would have been able to intercept his parents' killers! But then again she might have been decapitated as well; and he would have three heads at home in his freezer: two the size of joints of meat; and one the size of a potato. Doesn't bear thinking about.

The casino's Scandinavian-style decorated dog lounge was soundproofed so none of the dogs in there knew about the chaos that was happening in the main part of the complex until Chauncy threw open the doors. Upon hearing the alarm all the dogs looked up from their activities curiously, and that is when Chauncy caught a glimpse of something emerald: Marianne was in the dog lounge and she was walking confidently [how dare she!] towards a group of dogs of which Sadie was one of!

Sadie's face, which had seen Marianne, was terrified, and outraged.

Marianne's arms were extended in front of her and she was looming forwards in a way which made Chauncy think she was about to pick Sadie up, so he ran really fast into the lounge and floored her before she had the chance. [By flooring her I mean he grabbed her waist from behind and threw her out of the way.]

Sadie's face showed relief now, though only briefly because the loud alarm and pandemonium was now being felt by all canines in the Dog Lounge.

It was all right though, Chauncy just explained the situation to all of them and said how they needed to get out now. The smaller dogs ran and jumped on his shoulders while the bigger, older dogs followed him outside like he was Jesus.

Just as Chauncy and all the dogs got outside into the night air, a massive explosion went off inside the casino!

Chauncy knew, as a Navy Seal, that one explosion is sure to be followed by another. He needed to act fast to:

a) move all the people idling around in the car park to a safe distance away from the building,

and b) get back inside the casino to rescue the many souls who were still in there, trapped by fallen debris, and waiting to die.

Chauncy estimated he had about 8 minutes to sort all this out. He ran to his car, put Sadie in her car seat, and wrapped her in tin foil. "I'll be back soon, kiddo, then me and you can go home and tell Grandma and Grandpa [he thinks they're still alive, remember] what a brave girl you've been. But first, I've got a few things to do. Sit tight, girl."

Sadie wanted to stop him, but she knew that once he had his heart set on saving lives there was just no stopping him.

Chauncy ran over to one of the security guards, "I'm going back in. Don't try and stop me, man! There are people dying in there. The building is on fire, dammit! I don't know about you but I'm not prepared to stand back and watch. It goes against every thing I'm trained for," he paused, "as a human being."

And in he went.

As soon as Chauncy stepped back inside the burning building the heat hit him. Searing heat, like when you open the oven door to check on your Fray Bentos and it just hits you: boom!

He looked down at his t-shirt, made of tight sheer nylon, and knew he must take it off or it would melt to his skin. He caught sight of himself in a mirror, and saw the garment was already clinging to his upper torso with perspiration. He peeled it off gently while breathing in and out really fast. He knew he needed to slow himself down, it was all right being a hero but to run any further into this building breathing in and out at the speed that he was, well, it'd be insane!

He took a moment to centre himself, and to remember that in that monastery in France he had been to a seminar on improving strength of mind and lung capacity.

Soon he was ready to take in a big breath that would last up to 3 minutes, enabling him to avoid any toxic fumes and bits of plywood that might be in the air.

"Huuuuuuuuuu," he said [that's the sound

of breathing in] then he paused for what was
probably only a millionnth second but the
thing about Chauncy is he has the capacity to
experience time deeply, so he used that moment
very well, saying, "I am water, fire does not
work on me, for I am water," then, with his
breath comfortably held, he ran with all he
had through the burning building against all
the advice of any fire safety officer who
might have witnessed this scene, towards the
danger, towards the flames, in order to save
any life he could.

And then.

Through the smoke Chauncy caught sight of
something green. Emerald green. He stopped,
breath still held comfortably, and squinted.
She was slumped over an armchair. It was her
all right. He rolled his eyes.

      "She broke my heart in a million pieces,
left me without hope, with a gaping hole in my
chest where once there had been life! Where
once there had been a heart that wanted to
love, and now, I do not love anything apart
from Sadie and my parents and all the good
people and animals in the world for I am
damaged romantically! Never will I be fully

repaired, never again will I seek the love of a woman. Here now, in front of me, needing me, needing a kind heart, is the person whom obliterated mine. Well, I am not a monster. I may never love a woman again, but two wrongs don't make a right, and let me tell you now, I will pick this woman up, I will take her safety, but I will not hang around after that, I'm getting straight off — I can tell you that right now." [This is an excellent monologue and because of all the emotions that are covered it will probably become a popular auction piece for places like RADA.]

And so he bent down and picked Marianne up, who managed to be both limp and hefty at the same time, and he carried her out of the burning building without looking at her.

Once they were outside he left her in the care of the 'professionals', stopping only to say, "I hope I never see you again," which he said just as she opened her eyes so she definitely heard him.

Then he strode towards his car, to Sadie whom was making a lovely recovery, and they drove back to his parents' house, who if you remember had not long since been murdered, so Chauncy got home to find only their heads, one on each chair in the living room, for they had been decapitated, and their bodies were nowhere to be found.

CHAPTER 11

BACK TO THE PRESENT DAY

Chauncy says "I don't know about you, Sadie, but I'm not sure how useful remembering all that was in terms of finding out whom killed my parents. I think what I'll do is give the police a ring and see if they've had any new leads."

He looks at his mobile phone and hovers a finger over the key which would call Detective Inspector Cindy Barker, one of the detectives who'd been in charge of their murder case.

She was a good egg, no doubt about that, but there was only so much she could do. As she so often expressed, "Her hands were tied". Every time she said that both Chauncy and Sadie would sigh.

The other thing about her was that she used to look at Chauncy with what can only be described as desperation.

A few months after the murders, the case

had been declared "Officially closed, but with
the back door open," — and those were the
words not of Cindy Barker, oh no, she was too
by-the-book for that. Those words were spoken
by the other detective in charge of the case,
a man one, called John Rhino, whom Chauncy
liked very much. [For TV adaptation, if
available, an actor from The Bill should play
John Rhino, preferably one with asthma.]

John Rhino had that old school grit that you
just don't get in a policeman under 55. He'd
say things like, "I don't care, I'm retiring
soon," but what he meant was: *I don't care
about pissing a few people off so long as
justice is served.*

   He had a drinking problem, but a fun
one. One where if he arrived at work sober,
hair stuck up, one eye bigger than the other,
someone would pop to the Spar for a bottle of
rum to gee him along. Within 20 minutes he'd
emerge from his office, hair smooth and eyes
adjusted, sometimes singing a Frank Sinatra
number, ready to solve crimes.

   Naturally, his wife had left him years
ago, saying he was more married to his job
than her. She now lives with her new boyfriend
in a townhouse with character features and
tri-folding doors leading into the garden.

Also John Rhino has two grown up children whom he sees once a year for an awkward and self-conscious catch up.

The thing is, last year, John Rhino's big, bovine presence and his spontaneous, agitated demeanour, provided a useful distraction for the recently bereaved Chauncy who had, of course, had a huge shock, the kind of shock that would have turned his hair white if it wasn't already.

Depending on how you looked at it, in those weeks after the murders, you could either say that John Rhino became a father figure for Chauncy OR Chauncy became a surrogate son for John Rhino. John Rhino could have just phoned his actual son and taken an actual interest in his life, but oftentimes the simplest solution is the one we are too blindest to see. [Print on a t-shirt to wear at book launch, BBC Breakfast interviews etc]

Whatever your perspective, there was no denying that John Rhino did everything in his power to support Chauncy through his bereavement, such as getting a bit of money out of the petty cash tin at the station and taking him to strip clubs. It is important to know that because of Chauncy's ethics, Chauncy would keep his eyes closed during any stripping and he would also physically wretch if any of the women touched him.

So the two men were there for each other
for a brief time, and though Chauncy didn't
ever see John Rhino participating in any
detective work strictly per say, he did
appreciate some of his verbal encouragement
and views on grief and the loss of his
parents. He'd say things like, "They came here
to do what they needed to do, and now they've
fucked off again. They're in a better place
now — better than this shit hole, anyway."

So now, a year on, was it time for Chauncy to
get in touch with John Rhino again? Perhaps
with the passing of time he would have some
fresh insights? [Hm, yeah, I'm not sure.]

Chauncy decides to call John Rhino, who
answers after one ring, and says YES to seeing
Chauncy and insists they meet immediately, but
he's moved to the seaside, so can Chauncy
drive there ASAP please? It's an hour away but
Chauncy doesn't mind as he's got a new pair of
driving gloves to wear in. He decides it's
best to leave Sadie at home, so he drops her
off back at the penthouse, passing her to
Godfrey and then getting back into the car.

The meeting place, chosen by John Rhino,
is a cafe above a big jazzy arcade on the

seafront. You have to go up an escalator to
get to the cafe which makes Chauncy feel like
it's going to be nicer than it is. Chauncy is
there first, and he sits waiting at a table
made of formica with sticky stains on it.

Soon John Rhino arrives. He dances his
way off the escalator, then does a moonwalk
over to Chauncy's table. He's on friendly
terms with the staff, it seems, and shouts
"All right, treacle!" to the bored looking
women at the counter.

Chauncy is a bit taken aback by the
volume, but reassures himself it's just John
Rhino's jocular personality and joy de vivre
coming out.

However, once he's seated at the table
Chauncy realises that John Rhino is actually
just quite aggressive and erratic. When
Chauncy asks him if he's got any theories
about his parents' murder he says "NO! NO I
will not come out of retirement forward slash
redundancy, actually it was more like
indefinite suspension, but then that's what
happens to the truth-seekers! They're shut
down, mouths sown up, sent to one of the four
corners of the world and told to keep quiet,
well, I will not be shut down and my voice
WILL be heard!"

"Does that mean you will or you won't

help solve the murder with me?"

"Sorry I got carried away. I stick to my original answer. It's a no."

Anyway this scene ends with John Rhino grabbing Chauncy's hands and saying "Please, just £50, I'll give you hundred back, I swear." Chauncy gently takes £50 out of his wallet, leaves it on the table and says, "Take care of yourself, John Rhino."

[What we are seeing here is that Chauncy has become the father figure, John Rhino is the child, and when this is filmed for the telly it's one of those BOOM moments that will make people take to Twitter to share their theories about what is going on].

Chauncy then stands on the seafront staring out to sea in a scarf and a cagoule, thinking about how far he's come, emotionally. [Write to ITV about potential Broadchurch reboot?]

John Rhino can be seen in the background looking like he is at a pivotal crossroads in his life: he will either take that £50 to the bookies via the off licence, OR he'll start watching a lot of Youtube videos about spirituality, which will begin his awakening, and ultimately lead him to maybe join — but most likely start — a cult.

Anyway so John Rhino isn't going to be any help, and Chauncy just cannot bear the idea of calling Detective Inspector Cindy Barker so that's that.

He puts his snug gloves on, gets back in his car and drives back to his parents' house.

CHAPTER 12

Driving up to the house, Chauncy notices a staggeringly hot silhouette standing at the front door. *Who's that?* He wonders. *Oh, it's the other version of me from the parallel universe,* he realises.

On the one hand it's nice to see him, on the other he's very hard work.

While still in the car Chauncy rehearses what he'll say to Chauncy. Something like, "Look, I've had a long day and I'm very tired, very drained. If you could just pop back through your portal, that'd be great."

He sighs and takes his gloves off. Then he puts them back on. Then he gets out of the car.

As he walks through the garden gate he realises that the other Chauncy is wearing their bin bag and raspberry beret ensemble from Halloween '91!

He looks scandalous.

And what's that he's carrying? A spare bin bag. When Chauncy notices this he feels one of his chakras open.

"Hey, there you are!" says the other
Chauncy, gleefully. "I've been standing here
for hours. How are you? You look tired."

To be honest this small moment of
attention and kindness releases a torrent of
something inside of Chauncy, whom, as you
know, has had a very long day.

It is so nice to be… seen, he says non-
verbally.

"I'm here at your front door because,
well — I think we both know why I'm here. I
think we deserve to relive that Halloween
disco together, don't you? Growing up with the
amount of style and panache we had wasn't
easy. Imagine if we'd had each other for
support, like Bros, or the Proclaimers. Who
knows what could have happened." [Spin off
idea]

Chauncy sighs and says, "Yes, it would
have been terrific."

"So, what do you say… shall we… bro?"

Bro… oh what music that is! What deep
part of Chauncy doth that word waken and
trigger! "Yes!" he lisps.

"Right, you go and sellotape yourself
into that bin bag, and I'll fix us a drink,"

says the other Chauncy.

He seems different, more focused somehow. Like he's the kind of man who knows what he wants and isn't afraid to ask for it.

Chauncy opens the front door, and in they go. As Chauncy runs upstairs to his bedroom to get ready, the other Chauncy shouts, "I've already cut a hole in the bin bag for your head!"

"Nice one bro!"

Once he's in his bedroom, Chauncy strips, moisturisers, then covers himself in talc to absorb the moisturiser, then towels himself off to get rid of the talc, then sprays himself with the scent of 1991: Lynx Java.

Then he throws the bin bag up into the air and lets it fall onto his naked body. [Incredible.]

A few metres of sellotape later and he's ready to go.

He takes a deep breath at the top of the stairs and realises this is the happiest he has been in a very long time. The other Chauncy is waiting for him at the bottom of the stairs, where he watches him glide down, and they both think how he wouldn't be out of place on a curved staircase like what you find in stately homes.

"We look majestic," the other Chauncy says, whipping out a second raspberry beret [it's quite warm] from under his bin bag. He plonks it down onto Chauncy's head and then they head into the kitchen.

"Actually shall we go into the living room and move the settee so we can make up some dance routines?"

"Great idea! I'll get my Erasure albums."

They spend the next two hours choreographing themselves into some fantastic positions. Then they have a choc ice to cool off.

Feeling giddy, they fall back onto the settee together and Chauncy says, "I can show you my collection of porcelain pigs if you like. I've got about 23. Pig on a bench reading a newspaper, drunk pig, pig at the beach in a bikini…"

"Pig doing ballet in a lemon tutu…"

"Yes! How did you…? Oh, of course. I forget sometimes that we have so many of the same shared experiences. I suppose it would be boring for you… to see them."

"No," Chauncy turns to Chauncy, "it's

not that, it's just…"

They're quiet for a moment, because they are both thinking things. Probably about which pigs they've got etc. Then the other Chauncy breaks the silence by saying, "What about the rare and elusive pig wearing trilby, leather jacket and sunglasses — do you have that one?"

"Have I!"

"That's what I'm asking, have you?"

"Yes."

"Well then I would love to see that pig."

"Thank you," whispers Chauncy.

He takes a moment to take a mental photograph of this moment: the two of them squashed together on his dead mother's two-seater, sweating profusely inside bin bags, looking incredibly attractive, endorphins running amok. Of all the ways he imagined this day to end, this was not one of them.

"Shall we…?" Chauncy suggests.

"We shall," Chauncy confirms.

Then they stand up and waft their bin bags about to let some air in and up them, and up to the bedroom they go. Lovely.

To be continued...

... hopefully

I've had to take a break from writing because Chauncy has gone what can only be described as AWOL since that last scene.

WHERE ARE YOU??.?? CHAUNCY

As soon as he comes back and does his next night time visitation with me I will channel him once more and write more of this fantastic ground breaking literary novel.

COME ON CHAUNCY!!!!!

In the meantime I will make the most of his sabbatical by cracking on with some important book and publishing admin and so the last part of this book is made of:

- BONUS MATERIALS -

On the following pages you will find:
- Press release and sample of an interview with me
- FACTS about Chauncy
- Ideas for future books (by me)
- Letter to Aidan Turner RE: Poldark

Thank you, you're welcome

DRAFT OF A PRESS RELEASE FOR WHEN I'M A FAMOUS WRITER

SEND IT TO: High-brow broadsheet newspapers / culture magazines / New York Times etc.

SUBJECT: "BEST SELLING CRITICALLY ACCLAIMED WRITER IS AVAILABLE FOR INTERVIEWS, PROFILES, Q&As etc"

BRIEFLY, say something like:

Hello, I am the writer Bella De La Rocher and I've got a book coming out. Would you like to put something about it in your paper?

What follows is an example of the kind of article you'd have on your hands if you interviewed me about me being writer.

What I've done is imagined that I am a top journalist called Brendah whom is interviewing me (Bella De La Rocher).

Please note this is one of those interviews where they include observations about what the person is wearing and so on. Brendah is quite famous for it, actually. This is why she's a top journalist and why the paper she works for has chosen her to interview me.

So just to be clear the interview below is written from the interviewer's point of view (that's Brendah) but I've actually made it, and her, up.

Thank you.

Title suggestion, something like

"In A Writer's Den, I Find A Genius Armed With A Pen."

By Brendah Watermon

When I arrive at Bella De La Rocher's home, I'm greeted by a stunning sight: the writer is wearing a mustard tunic over turquoise tights, and her head is topped with a mortar board. Though she has never been to university, De La Rocher wishes to use her platform to break down class barriers. She has earrings in her ears which are made of a lot of different coloured buttons. The effect is somehow both elaborate and down to earth. Most of all it is creative, and that is what this woman obviously is.

She shows me into her writing room and ushers me into a wicker chair. I get my reporters notebook out and ready myself.

"So, Bella!" I begin, my voice a bit too loud, because I am nervous, "Tell us about your journey as writer."

De La Rocher takes a deep breath and laughs on the exhale, as if to say both, *How long have you got?* and also: *It happened in a heartbeat.* I give her a moment to collect her thoughts and as she does this I have a look around the room we are in.

I wanted the interview to take place in De La Rocher's natural habitat, in order to really get a feel for how she creates, so I have travelled to Doncaster where she lives in an annex not attached to her parents' house. Despite there being a clear 5 inch gap between the annex and the house her parents choose to reside in, Bella is often mistaken for someone who still lives at home, which is very much not the case.

I decide to temporarily shelf the question about how she became writer, it was probably too big of a concept to just throw out there, and I should have known better as a top journalist. I realise I must change track so I ask about the annex instead.

"Did this used to be…"

"A free-standing garage, yes. It's funny really because everyone thinks I still live with my parents, just because I can't physically get into my property without going into theirs first, and then using their kitchen side door to step over the 5 inch gap to get through my side door. While yes, there is a pull-up garage door I *could* use, I don't like using it because it makes me feel like I live in a garage! And I don't."

I look around and understand perfectly, because this is definitely not a garage: it is a studio apartment, albeit one without a kitchen or a bathroom. Again, these are all accessed via her parents' house but add zero weight to the argument that she still lives at home. She does, however, have a fridge freezer, a kettle, a water cooler, and a camping stove, and a bucket, so really she doesn't have to go into her parents' house ever if she chooses not to, so why is everyone so bothered about it anyway?! It beggars belief, it really, really does.

"How about you ask me about something I have created?" inserts De La Rocher, before going on to also say, "You seem to have got side-tracked by my living arrangements and frankly — it's weird."

She's absolutely right, of course. I take a breath. "Is it true that you are also a poet, as well as a novelist?" I ask.

De La Rocher closes her eyes and nods. It's a very powerful moment, while also being very real.

Perhaps the most famous of De La Rocher's poems is *The Fox* which was the first poem to ever be read out in the Houses Of Parliament.

It's what you might call a very 'primeval' poem which to the untrained eye seems to be about fox hunting, but the fox is actually representative of not only minority groups but also the British preoccupation with having holidays abroad.

When Jeremy Corbyn read the poem out loud in the Houses of Parliament, he said it encapsulated the spirit of the times perfectly and also he wishes he'd heard it before the last election because it would have been the inspiration for his entire manifesto.

I put this to De La Rocher, and she leans forward, as if she has suddenly been dynamically galvanised by politics and art. "If I were to eat a banana, would it not weep?" she asks, and I'm perplexed, dumb-founded, unsure of how to answer. "We're genetically very similar to bananas," she continues, "and yet — do we take care of them, the bananas? Or do we simply peel them, discard their clothes, pulverise their innards?"

It's startling for me to be involved in such an intense conversation and I am not ashamed to admit I'm out of my depth here. De La Rocher senses this and her indisputable capacity to be human resurfaces. "I'm sorry," she says, "it is just so hard being writer, being voice. As I am voice to so many items, causes, in fact — entire worlds — and it is exhausting — and yet … I wouldn't have it any other way."

I see this as my cue to end the interview, which has been one of the most enlightening ones I've ever done.

I pick up my reporter's notebook and retreat backwards, out of the dark, lava-lamp-lit annex, through her parents' kitchen (it's Mince Monday) and into the hallway and out — out the front door and into the light — challenged, ruffled, confused — and forever changed.

When I'm back in my office on Fleet Street, I reflect on how I really wished I'd taken a film crew with me because it would have made a great segment for a late night arts show. I think it would have worked well mostly filmed in colour to make the most of Bella's outfit, rugs, lava lamps and so on, but then interspersed with close ups of her profile, hands pulling on bits of thread off of a scarf, close up on mortar board tassle and so on, and those shots would be in black and white and on a shaky handheld camera.

If only I'd thought of it before. OH WELL YOU DIDN'T DID YOU BRENDAH, I say out loud to myself, chastisingly.

That is THE END of the interview sample and also the press release.

SOME FACTS about Chauncy

Re: leather jackets: Chauncy has 27 of these; for he has bought one every year of his life since he was 6 years old. His current favourite is the dove grey one which is studded, cropped, and sleeveless.

Chauncy is so enigmatic that he can stand in the doorway of any Starbucks and after so long everyone — and I mean everyone — in that Starbucks will turn to look at him.

His favourite smell is parsnips, and he's developing an aftershave of it.

Chauncy is the only man who can wear tap shoes in a non-tapping context and pull it off. He is actually experimenting with a new look: cropped trousers and tap shoes.

When Chauncy has a headache, he prefers to allow a paracetamol to dissolve slowly on his tongue.

Additionally: Chauncy knows if you take a vitamin tablet at the same time as a paracetamol it turbo charges it.

Chauncy is the kind of man who can do spreadsheets but

never, ever will. He prefers to keep up his important accounts etc by recording himself talking about them onto a cassette.

FUTURE BOOK AND TV SERIES IDEAS

ALL WITH ALLITERATIVE TITLES

MOSTLY* FEATURING CHAUNCY

CHAUNCY'S CHAKRAS: An access-all-areas look into Chauncy's spiritual body.

Notes: Would also be good TV series / travelogue: journeying with Chauncy to sacred places around the world etc AND journeying within his insides. Using a mini camera like when you have an endoscopy.

CHAUNCY'S CHAPATIS: A niche cookery book with lots of photos of Chauncy wearing an apron.

Notes: Title also works with CHICKPEAS

CHAUNCY'S CHIMNEYS: Historical inspection of chimneys. Mostly chimneys in stately homes. Includes lots of photos of Chauncy dusted with soot.

CHAUNCY'S CHECKOUT: This is a beautiful coffee table book with lots of photos of the contents of Chauncy's shopping basket

CHAUNCY'S CHILBLAINS: Chauncy travels to the Arctic in an unsuitable outfit THIS IS THE up close & personal illustrated story of his recovery

CHAUNCY'S CHECK-UPS: An encyclopaedic catalogue of Chauncy's medical history. Illustrated.

* All

LETTER

TO: AIDAN TURNER

FROM: THE BBC

RE: NEXT SERIES OF POLDARK

Hello Aidan

This is the BBC. I am pleased to inform you that we have decided to keep on making the television series Poldark, and we would like you to come back in your role as the main character Ross Poldark, the brooding, be-hatted 1790s gent with a demi-wave.

HOWEVER. You may have heard a rumour that the role has been re-cast to a certain Chauncy Nathaniel Swanston, and in a way it has.

HOWEVER what we want you to do is play Ross as if you are Chauncy playing Ross.

Does that make sense? If not, just re-read that sentence again.

Have you got it now? Excellent.

The main thing you need to know is that you will have a new wig (it is white) and some new eyes (they are green). Your jawline can stay exactly as it is. Your best friend is no longer that doctor whom you went to France to save, it is now a chiwawa called Sadie. This is now the most important relationship you will have with another cast member and you will be asked to do some extra acting classes to ensure you can act alongside a canine.

When you receive the scripts for the next series you will notice they have been annotated by the writer Bella De La Rocher whom is now in charge of POLDARK.

Thank 'ee Capn Raaws.

The BBC.

THE END

of this particular book,

but I will definitely write more books

Acknowledgements:

Just me and Chauncy, thanks.

If he ever comes back! hahahahahaahahh

THANK YOU

Allow me to thank you, dear reader, for being here, and taking this joyous ride with me. Yes, it was a gamble. Yes, it was very brave of me to publish a work-in-progress but as writer I must, _must_, take risks and push boundaries.

Have you enjoyed the book? If so, why not tell me via social media, or leave a review, or tell someone else? Not because I need you to - because I don't - I'm actually very fulfilled and confident thanks, but just because it will help other readers find me and that will be really nice for them.

Earnestly, I thank you from deep within for playing such a significant part in this book becoming a bestselling critically acclaimed commercial and cult success.

YOU'RE WELCOME,

Bella De La Rocher